Stars and Stripes and Soldiers

Written and illustrated by
RICHARD ROSENBLUM

SCHOLASTIC INC.
New York Toronto London Auckland Sydney

To the old regiment

Acknowledgments

The author gratefully acknowledges the invaluable assistance of Michael J. McAfee, Curator of History, West Point Museum. Thanks also to Lieutenant Colonel Martin Andresen of the U.S. Military History Research Institute for reviewing the text and drawings.

ISBN 0–590–45222–3

12 11 10 9 8 7 6 5 4 3 2 1   3 4 5 6 7 8/9

Printed in the U.S.A.   08

First Scholastic printing, April 1993

Introduction

Many countries have flags that are red, white, and blue — but there is only one "Stars and Stripes."

This book shows you how the national flag of the United States changed as the country grew from the original thirteen states to fifty. It shows you other flags, too, that mark important events in U.S. history.

Just as the flag changed, so did the uniforms of the fighting forces that have helped keep the United States free and independent for more than 200 years. The uniforms shown in these pictures give you a good idea of how American soldiers dressed, from Colonial times to the 1990s.

THE BRITISH UNION FLAG

The French and Indian War was a war between England and France that was fought in part of North America.

At the time, the North American colonies were part of the British Empire, ruled by the king of England, and France had colonies in Canada. Both countries were after more land to colonize.

Many North American Indians fought with the French. Most colonists fought with the British under the British Union flag, also called the Union Jack.

American colonists fought in their own regiments. Rogers' Rangers was made up of expert frontier fighters led by Major Robert Rogers. They wore their own distinctive green uniforms.

THE BUNKER HILL FLAG

The Battle of Bunker Hill was one of the earliest battles of the American Revolution, the war with which the thirteen American colonies won their independence from England.

The Colonial soldiers called themselves minutemen. Under the command of General William Prescott, they had built forts on a group of hills surrounding the city of Boston.

On June 17, 1775, the British Army attacked the forts on Breed's Hill. The British marched up the hill twice. The minutemen fought them off both times. But on the third charge, the minutemen ran out of gunpowder and had to retreat.

Even though fought on Breed's Hill, this battle has always been called the Battle of Bunker Hill, which was actually located nearby.

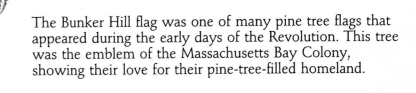

The Bunker Hill flag was one of many pine tree flags that appeared during the early days of the Revolution. This tree was the emblem of the Massachusetts Bay Colony, showing their love for their pine-tree-filled homeland.

Navy Jack

Gadsden Flag

Culpepper Flag

The American Revolutionary War, 1775–1781

RATTLESNAKE FLAGS

During the Revolution there were many versions of a flag designed with a rattlesnake and the words, "Don't tread on me." The Culpepper Minutemen from Virginia carried one.

The Gadsden Flag was another rattlesnake flag, and a Navy Jack version flew over ships of the Massachusetts and North Carolina navies.

The American Revolutionary War, 1775–1781

THE MOULTRIE FLAG

While defending Charleston, South Carolina, in 1776, Colonel William Moultrie and his 375 Regulars flew this flag over Fort Sullivan. Their defense of the fort forced the British attackers to withdraw and saved the southern colonies from invasion.

The design of this flag was suggested by the blue of the soldiers' uniforms and the silver crescents the men wore on their caps, which were inscribed with the words, "liberty or death."

THE BENNINGTON FLAG

Fort Bennington, in Vermont, was occupied by Colonial soldiers called the Green Mountain Boys, organized by Ethan Allen. With Seth Warner leading them, they successfully defended the fort against attacks by British forces.

The Bennington flag may have been the model for the Stars and Stripes that later became the flag for the new nation of the United States of America. Or, as some historians now believe, it may have been created in 1876 for the Centennial celebration.

The American Revolutionary War, 1775–1781
THE STARS AND STRIPES

On July 4, 1776, the thirteen colonies declared themselves free and independent states—the United States of America. On June 14, 1777, the Continental Congress authorized a national flag. It became known as the Stars and Stripes.

This was the flag that the soldiers of the Revolutionary Army carried during their great victory at Saratoga and throughout the terrible winter at Valley Forge.

The flag finally waved triumphantly at Yorktown, Virginia, on October 19, 1781, when General George Washington accepted the surrender of General Charles Cornwallis and the British Army.

There were thirteen stars and thirteen stripes on the national flag to represent the thirteen original colonies.

A popular story is that the first Stars and Stripes was made by Betsy Ross, a flag-maker in Philadelphia at the time of the Revolution, but there is no proof this story is true.

THE STAR-SPANGLED BANNER

In 1812, the United States again went to war against the British to defend their liberty. The war ended when the British and the Americans signed the Treaty of Ghent in Ghent, Belgium, on December 24, 1814.

The flag of 1812 had fifteen stars and strips because two new states—Kentucky and Vermont—had joined the Union by then.

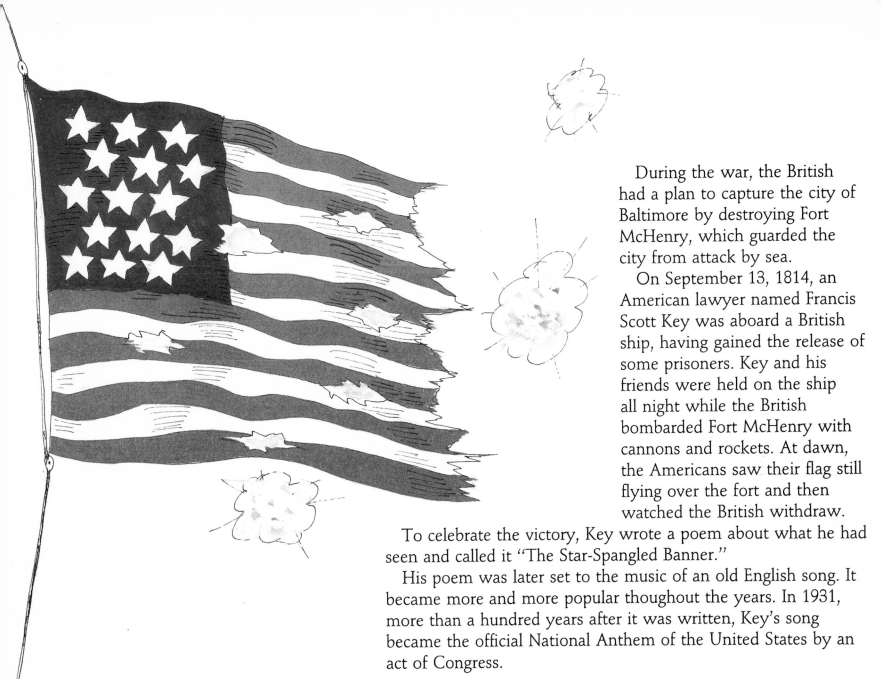

During the war, the British had a plan to capture the city of Baltimore by destroying Fort McHenry, which guarded the city from attack by sea.

On September 13, 1814, an American lawyer named Francis Scott Key was aboard a British ship, having gained the release of some prisoners. Key and his friends were held on the ship all night while the British bombarded Fort McHenry with cannons and rockets. At dawn, the Americans saw their flag still flying over the fort and then watched the British withdraw.

To celebrate the victory, Key wrote a poem about what he had seen and called it "The Star-Spangled Banner."

His poem was later set to the music of an old English song. It became more and more popular thoughout the years. In 1931, more than a hundred years after it was written, Key's song became the official National Anthem of the United States by an act of Congress.

The 20-STAR FLAG

By 1818, five more states had been admitted to the Union, making the total now twenty. The new states were Tennessee, Ohio, Louisiana, Indiana, and Mississippi. Congress agreed that it would be impractical to continue adding stripes and stars to the flag. They decided to go back to thirteen stripes, which would stand for the original thirteen colonies, and have a star for each state.

The Great Star Flag showed twenty stars arranged to form one large star. Other flags showed the stars in a circle or in rows.

Since no special kind of star was designated, the five-pointed star became the regular star through custom. And because there was no official rule about how the stars should be arranged, there were many different designs.

It was not until 1912 that the arrangement of rows was selected as the permanent design.

THE ALAMO FLAG

The Battle of the Alamo took place in what is now San Antonio, Texas.

Since 1824, Texas had been a free state in the federal republic of Mexico, and thousands of Americans had settled there. But in 1835, a Mexican general named Santa Anna took over the government as dictator, and war broke out. Texans fought to keep their republic.

In February of 1836, General Santa Anna and an army of 2,000 attacked a group of Americans defending an old Spanish mission called the Alamo. There were only 183 Americans in the Alamo, and all of them—including the famous pioneers William Travis, James Bowie, and Davy Crockett—were killed in the thirteen-day battle. "Remember the Alamo!" became the battle cry in the fight for Texas independence.

The flag that was flown on the Alamo was that of the Republic of Texas, established twelve years before the Battle of the Alamo.

THE LONE STAR FLAG

After the Alamo, the Americans in Texas pressed harder for independence. On April 21, 1836, General Sam Houston and his Texas army defeated General Santa Anna at San Jacinto, and Texas became a free republic.

The Texans adopted a national flag with two large stripes and one large star. Because there was just one star, it was called the Lone Star Flag.

Texas joined the Union in 1845 to become the twenty-eighth state. It is called the Lone Star State after its first flag, which is also its state flag.

THE PATHFINDER FLAG

General John C. Frémont, nicknamed "the Pathfinder," was a famous American explorer.

In 1842, the U.S. government sent him and his men to explore the land beyond the Missouri River. Their job was to determine which routes the wagon trains should use on their way west. The famous pioneer scout Kit Carson was Frémont's guide on this trip.

Frémont designed a flag for the expedition, which came to be known as the Pathfinder Flag. Frémont took it with him as he made his way up the Wind River Mountains in Wyoming and planted it on top of the highest mountain. The mountain was named Frémont Peak after him.

The twenty-eight stars in Frémont's flag surround an eagle clutching arrows in one claw and—as a sign of friendship—a peace pipe in the other.

THE 28-STAR FLAG

In 1845, the United States decided to admit Texas to the Union. Mexico did not like the idea, and there were battles along the U.S.–Mexican border.

In May of 1846, President James Polk signed a bill declaring war against Mexico. American forces entered Mexico and fought many battles, including ones at Buena Vista and Vera Cruz.

The final American victory at Chapultepec led to the fall of Mexico City.

The Mexican War inspired a famous line in the "Marine Hymn," the official song of the United States Marines. "From the Halls of Montezuma" refers to Montezuma II, the last Aztec emperor of Mexico.

Many U.S. regiments carried their own flag. These men carry the colors of the United States 8th Infantry Regiment.

DRAGOON GUIDON

In June of 1846, Colonel Stephen Kearney left Fort Leavenworth, Kansas, with a force of Missouri volunteers and regular army dragoons—heavily armed mounted soldiers (cavalry).

After a long march down the old Santa Fe Trail, they captured the city of Santa Fe. Leaving the Missouri Volunteers behind to occupy the city, Kearney and his dragoons, led by Kit Carson, marched another 900 miles through mountain passes and deserts into southern California. There they helped defeat a Mexican army at the San Gabriel River and went on to occupy Los Angeles.

Riders in the 1st Dragoons carry
their regimental banner into battle.

THE STARS AND BARS

The Civil War began when a group of southern states withdrew from the Union to form their own nation, which they called the Confederate States of America. In March of 1861, they adopted a flag with seven stars, one for each state that had left the Union. (Four more states would join later.)

The northern states wanted to preserve the Union and, in April, war broke out between the two parts of the country. During this time, people in the North were called "Yankees." People in the South were known as "Rebels."

Each of the Confederate States and militias adopted and designed their own uniforms in different shades of gray. Some were simple and some were fancy.

THE REBEL BATTLE FLAG

The first time the Rebels flew the Stars and Bars in battle was at Bull Run on July 21, 1861. They discovered that in the smoke and confusion of battle their flag looked too much like the Union Stars and Stripes, especially when it hung limp.

They designed a new battle flag. In 1863 a version of this flag became the official flag of the Confederate States.

The Rebel Battle Flag is carried here by troopers of General Jeb Stuart's 1st Virginia Cavalry.

THE 33-STAR FLAG

At the beginning of the Civil War, there were many special volunteer units of the Northern Army. One group of soldiers dressed in colorful uniforms made up of baggy pants, a fancy vest, and a red turban hat called a *fez*. The uniforms were modeled after those worn by French–Algerian infantry—*Zouaves*.

These Union soldiers also called themselves *Zouaves*. Some units, such as the 5th New York Volunteers, wore the uniforms into battle.

Throughout the war, the Union armies carried the traditional Stars and Stripes, with a star for every state.

THE 54TH MASSACHUSETTS REGIMENTAL FLAG

The 54th Massachusetts Regiment was the first all-black infantry unit to fight in the Civil War.

The regiment won honor and glory when it tried to take the Southern stronghold at Fort Wagner in South Carolina. Although the attack did not succeed, the bravery of these soldiers paved the way for two hundred thousand black soldiers to fight on the Union side.

By 1863, Kansas and West Virginia had joined the Union and two more stars were added to the flag for a total of thirty-five.

THE 35-STAR CAVALRY GUIDON

From the time of the Mexican War, there were always regular United States Cavalry units, called Horse Soldiers, on the frontiers. Their mission was to protect people settling in the West from attacks by the North American Indians, who were trying to preserve their ancestral lands from these invasions.

During this period, the army built small, isolated forts to serve as headquarters for the cavalry. Some of the most famous are Forts Riley and Leavenworth in Kansas, and Fort Dodge in Iowa, and Fort Laramie in Wyoming.

Horse Soldiers carried a cavalry guidon, a small flag with a V-shaped tail, when they rode into battle.

THE 10TH CAVALRY REGIMENTAL FLAG

The 9th and 10th Regular Cavalry Regiments, authorized by Congress in 1866, were regiments of black enlisted men. They were stationed in Texas and New Mexico and campaigned all over the Southwest. The Indians called the black cavalrymen "buffalo soldiers."

These 1889 10th Cavalry troopers are shown in their "dress blues."

As of 1885, regimental flags of the cavalry are always yellow. Infantry regimental flags are always blue. Artillery flags are red.

THE 45-STAR FLAG

In February of 1898, the battleship U.S.S. *Maine* was blown up in the harbor of Havana, Cuba. Blaming the Spanish, who occupied the country, the United States sent an army to Cuba. In April, Spain declared war.

The Spanish-American War was very brief. The U.S. Army, in spite of late-arriving supplies, defeated the even less well-off Spanish Army within a few months.

The most famous battle of the war was at a place called San Juan Hill. Colonel Theodore Roosevelt led his regiment of 1st United States Voluntary Cavalry on a famous *dis*mounted charge because their horses had not arrived from the States.

In their successful charge uphill, Roosevelt's men carried the United States flag, which at that time had forty-five stars.

Roosevelt's regiment was nick-named the "Rough Riders." During the battle of San Juan Hill, they had help from the "Buffalo Soldiers" of the 9th United States Regular Cavalry, who were not given credit until many years later.

1910 WEST POINT COLOR GUARD WITH 46-STAR FLAG

The United States Military Academy at West Point, New York, was established in 1802. Their uniform has been "cadet gray" ever since the War of 1812, when there was a shortage of the deep-blue dye used in the original uniforms. The version worn today dates back to 1899.

This color guard of 1910 carries the United States Military Academy flag, adopted in 1902. About the only thing that's changed is the number of stars in the U.S. flag.

West Point uniforms have fancy jackets with three rows of brass buttons down the front, connected by double rows of black braid. The cap is leather, with a plume and a brass plate inscribed with the Academy insignia.

THE 48-STAR FLAG

A great war started in Europe in 1914. France, England, and Russia (the Allies) went to war against the Central Powers of Germany and Austria–Hungary. Many other nations soon became involved. It came to be known as World War I.

This war was different in many ways from all previous wars because it was fought with new, much more destructive weapons, such as tanks, airplanes, submarines, machine guns, and poison gas.

The United States joined the Allies in August of 1917. An American Expeditionary Force, under the command of General John Pershing, was sent to Europe. American soldiers—doughboys—participated in the great battles and victories at Chateau-Thierry, Belleau Wood, and the Argonne Forest.

Infantryman (doughboy)
Sailor
Army Air Corps pilot
Army nurse

THE 48-STAR FLAG

After a sneak attack by the Japanese on the United States Naval base at Pearl Harbor on December 7, 1941, American forces entered a second World War. The war had started in Europe in 1939.

With former allies England and France, the United States fought the Axis Powers of Germany, Italy, and Japan.

Naval battles were fought all over the Atlantic and Pacific oceans; there were tank battles in the North African desert, and air battles over the major cities of Europe and Asia.

In the campaign to free Europe from Axis control, the Allies invaded Sicily, Italy, and finally, on June 6, 1944 (D-Day), the beaches of Normandy, France.

World War II ended in 1945 with the unconditional surrender of Germany (in May) and Japan (in August).

American soldiers called themselves "G.I.'s" —an abbreviation of Government Issue.

G.I. paratroopers of the 82nd Airborne Division wear American flag patches on their right shoulders.

THE UNITED NATIONS FLAG

After World War II, Korea was divided into two separate countries. The northern part was governed by Communists and the southern part was a republic.

On June 2, 1950, the North Koreans invaded South Korea. The United Nations met and voted to raise an army to resist the invasion.

The United States was one of the seventeen nations, including South Korea, that volunteered to send troops for that army. It was the first time in U.S. history that American soldiers fought under another flag.

After many casualties, the war ended in an armistice that was worked out in 1953.

Women of the military:
Army (WAC)
Marines
Navy (WAVE)

THE 50-STAR FLAG

In 1965, the United States became involved in a long guerrilla war in Southeast Asia. The American government sent troops to help the government of South Vietnam from being taken over by the Communist Viet Cong, which ruled the north.

American involvement in the war lasted for ten years, and ended in 1975 with the withdrawal of U.S. forces.

In Vietnam, the United States fought under the new fifty-star flag. Alaska and Hawaii had become states in 1959.

Specially trained soldiers, called "Green Berets," fought in Vietnam.

Regular army infantrymen called themselves "Grunts."

THE 50-STAR FLAG

The Gulf War was a very brief war. It lasted from January 16, 1991, to midnight February 27, 1991. It was fought in the Middle East in countries bordering the Persian Gulf.

Iraq had invaded the neighboring country of Kuwait, a small but wealthy supplier of oil to the United States and other countries of the world. The United Nations ordered Iraq to leave Kuwait, but the Iraqi government refused.

The United States, together with other U.N. members, sent a force to the Arabian desert to press for Kuwait's release, and war broke out. With superior air power, the United States and its allies succeeded in liberating Kuwait.

United States servicemen and women wore battle uniforms especially designed for camouflage in the desert.